Thirteen Moons on Turtle's Back

A NATIVE AMERICAN YEAR OF MOONS

JOSEPH BRUCHAC and
JONATHAN LONDON

illustrated by
THOMAS LOCKER

A TRUMPET CLUB SPECIAL EDITION

To the children of Turtle Island

ISBN 0-590-99508-1

Text copyright © 1992 by Joseph Bruchac and Jonathan London. Illustrations copyright © 1992 by Thomas Locker, Inc. All rights reserved. Published by Scholastic Inc., 555 Broadway, New York, NY 10012, by arrangement with Philomel Books, a division of The Putnam & Grosset Group. TRUMPET and the TRUMPET logo are registered trademarks of Scholastic Inc.

12 11 10 9 8 7 6   8 9/9 0 1/0

Printed in the U.S.A.
First Scholastic printing, September 1996

Grandfather leaned over the long spruce log. The small boy stood close, waiting for the old man to notice him.

Grandfather looked up, a small smile on his face.

"*Kway*, Sozap," he said, "you do well at watching. Come closer. See now what I have done."

Sozap reached up to touch the carved shape of Turtle.

"How many scales are on Old Turtle's back?" Grandfather said. "*Kina*, look."

Sozap counted with care.

"Thirteen," he answered.

"*Unh-hunh!*" Grandfather said, "There are always thirteen on Old Turtle's back and there are always thirteen moons in each year. Many people do not know this. They do not know, as we Abenaki know, that each moon has its own name and every moon has its own stories. I learned those stories from my grandfather. Someday, Grandson, if your memory is as sharp as your eyes, you will be able to tell them to your grandchildren."

"Grandfather," Sozap said, "do other Native people have moons, too?"

The old man nodded. "Yes, Grandson."

Moon
of Popping Trees

Outside the lodge,
the night air is bitter cold.
Now the Frost Giant walks
with his club in his hand.
When he strikes the trunks
of the cottonwood trees
we hear them crack
beneath the blow.
The people hide inside
when they hear that sound.

But Coyote, the wise one,
learned the giant's
magic song,
and when Coyote sang it,
the Frost Giant slept.

Now when the cottonwoods
crack with frost again
our children know, unless
they hear Coyote's song,
they must stay inside,
where the fire is bright
and buffalo robes
keep us warm.

FIRST MOON   *Northern Cheyenne*

Baby Bear Moon

Long ago a small child
was lost in the snow.
We thought she had frozen,
but when spring came again,
she was seen with a mother bear
and her small cubs.

She had slept
all through the winter
with them, and from then on
the bears were her family
and her friends.

When we walk by on our snowshoes
we will not bother a bear
or her babies. Instead
we think how those small bears
are like our children.
We let them dream together.

SECOND MOON   *Potawatomi*

Maple Sugar Moon

Long ago maple syrup
dripped, thick from the trees.
All year round, you just had
to break a twig and lie down
beneath the tree with open mouth.

But the people got lazy
and when Our Creator,
Git-chee Ma-ni-tou,
sent his helper, Man-a-bo-zho,
to visit, he found
their village deserted
and all the people asleep
under the maple trees.

So he poured much water
into all the maples
so that now the people
would have to wake up,
make fires and boil down
the sap to make syrup.
They would have to work hard,
for that maple sap would flow
just this one time of the year,
the time we now call
Maple Sugar Moon.

THIRD MOON *Anishinabe*

Frog Moon

When the world was young,
Wis-a-ked-jak, the Trickster,
met with all of the animals
to decide how many moons
would be winter.

Moose answered,
"There should be as many
moons of winter
as hairs on my body."
Amik, the beaver,
said, "There should be
as many winter moons
as scales on my tail!"
Then O-ma-ka-ki, the little frog,
said, "There should only be
as many moons of snow
as toes on my foot."

Wis-a-ked-jak decided
that this was right.
So it is that winter
lasts only five moons,
and when it ends,
the small frogs sing
their victory song
in this moon with their name.

FOURTH MOON   *Cree*

Budding Moon

One year Old Man Winter
refused to leave our land,
and so our people asked for help
from our great friend, Ju-ske-ha,
known to some as the Sun.
He knocked on the door
of Winter's lodge
then entered and sat
by Winter's cold fire.

"Leave here or you will freeze,"
Winter said,
but Ju-ske-ha breathed
and Winter grew smaller.
Ju-ske-ha waved his hand
and a white owl flew down
to carry Winter
back to the deep snow
of the north.

The lodge melted away
and the trees turned green
with new buds
as the birds began to sing.
And where the cold fire
of winter had been
was a circle of white May flowers.
So it happens each spring
when the Budding Moon comes.
All the animals wake
and we follow them
across our wide, beautiful land.

FIFTH MOON *Huron*

Strawberry Moon

In late spring
a small boy
whose parents had died
went hunting game
down by the river
where the Jo-ge-oh,
the Little People who care
for the plants, live.

He shared what he caught
with those Little People.
In return they took him
in a magic canoe
up into the cliffs,
taught him many things
and gave him strawberries.

He was gone just four days,
but when he returned
years had passed
and he was a tall man.
He shared with his people
what he was taught and
gave them the sweetness
of the red strawberries.
So, each year, the Senecas
sing songs of praise
to the Little People,
thanking them again
for this moon's gift.

SIXTH MOON *Seneca*

Moon When
Acorns Appear

When the world was new
it was covered with water
until Earth Elder, the Creator,
reached down to
the mud below and placed it
up onto Turtle's back.
Earth Elder shaped
the sun and the stars,
then sat for a moment,
thinking of what was most needed,
what would help the humans
still to come.

That was when Earth Elder
made the first tree,
a great oak with twelve branches
arching over the land.
Then, sitting down beneath it,
the sun shining bright,
Earth Elder thought
of food for the people,
and acorns began to form.

So it is, each year,
when the sun shines brightest
these first acorns come
and our Pomo people
gather this moon's coming harvest.

SEVENTH MOON   *Pomo*

Moon of Wild Rice

In the old days, they say,
Bear came out of the ground
and became a man, but he was lonely.
He called to the sky:
"Thunder Eagle, come down
to earth and be my brother."
Then the giant Eagle,
who made thunder and lightning
by flapping his wings
and flashing his eyes,
flew down and he, too, became human.

Then the Creator, the Good Mystery,
made the Thunder People
the water-bearers, gave them
the gifts of corn and fire.
To the People of the Bear,
the Good Mystery gave
another gift—wild rice.

When the Thunder People came to visit
the Bear village near the mouth
of the Me-nom-i-nee River,
they brought with them water
and fire and corn.
The Bear People
gave them wild rice in exchange.
And so it came to be that
those two families live together
and harvest this special food
in the Wild Rice Moon.

EIGHTH MOON *Menominee*

Moose-Calling Moon

In this season when leaves
begin to turn color,
we go down to the lakes
and with birch-bark horns
make that sound which echoes
through the spruce trees,
the call of a moose
looking for a mate:
Mooo-ahhh-ahhh
Mooo-ahhh-ahhh.

If we wait there,
patient in our canoes,
the Moose will come.
His great horns are flat
because, long ago,
before people came,
Gloos-kap asked the Moose
what he would do
when he saw human beings.
"I will throw them up high
on my sharp horns," Moose said.

So Gloos-kap pushed his horns
flatter and made him smaller.
"Now, Moose," he said, "you will not
want to harm my people."
So the Moose comes and stands,
strong as the northeast wind.
He looks at us, then
we watch him disappear
back into the willows again.

NINTH MOON   *Micmac*

Moon of Falling Leaves

Long ago, the trees were told
they must stay awake
seven days and nights,
but only the cedar,
the pine and the spruce
stayed awake until
that seventh night.
The reward they were given
was to always be green,
while all the other trees
must shed their leaves.

So, each autumn, the leaves
of the sleeping trees fall.
They cover the floor
of our woodlands with colors
as bright as the flowers
that come with the spring.
The leaves return the strength
of one more year's growth
to the earth.

This journey
the leaves are taking
is part of that great circle
which holds us all close to the earth.

TENTH MOON   *Cherokee*

Moon When Deer Drop Their Horns

Now is the time when all the deer
must band together
in their winter lodges.
All autumn the bucks
fight with each other,
each one seeking to prove
himself stronger, each wanting
to be the chief of his people.

At one time the deer
kept their horns all year,
but when they entered
those winter lodges
the bucks continued
to fight with each other.
Earth Maker seeing
how the deer suffered
sent Na-na-bush, his helper,
to loosen the horns
from their foreheads
in this moon of late autumn.

Now, each winter,
when the deer gather,
just as we enter
our medicine lodges,
they leave their weapons
outside the door.
Their horns drop onto earth,
white with peaceful snow.

ELEVENTH MOON *Winnebago*

Moon
When Wolves
Run Together

Long ago, an old wolf
came to that time
when his life on earth
could last no longer.
"My people," he said,
"you can follow my footsteps
when the time comes for you
to join me in the skyland."
Then he left the earth,
climbing higher and higher,
and each place he stepped
the sky filled with stars.

Shunk man-i-tu tan-ka,
we call the wolves,
the powerful spirits
who look like dogs.
When they climb the hills
to lift their heads and sing
toward that road of stars,
their songs grow stronger
as they join their voices.

So, in this moon, we climb the hills,
lift our eyes toward the Wolf Trail
and remember that our lives
and songs are stronger
when we are together.

TWELFTH MOON   *Lakota Sioux*

Big Moon

The elders say our land
was shaped by Oh-zee-ho-zo,
the Changer, who formed himself
out of the dust which fell
from Creator's hands
after making the world.
He pushed against
the earth to rise
and great mountains rose up
on either side.
Then the waters flowed into
the place where he stood
and made Lake Champlain,
the lake we call Peh-ton-ba-gok,
the waters between.

When Oh-zee-ho-zo's travels
on this earth were done,
he came back to rest
by this lake once again,
making the circle complete.

So it is that our own
People of the Dawn
place one final moon
at the end of each cycle.
We call it Kit-chee Kee-sos, Big Moon.
Its name is the last
in our circle of seasons,
thirteen moons
on Old Turtle's back.

THIRTEENTH MOON   *Abenaki*

A note about this book

The native people of North America have always depended upon the natural world for their survival. Watching the changes going on in the natural world with each season, they also look up into the sky and see it changing. In many parts of North America, the native people relate the cycles of the moon (called Grandmother Moon by many Native Americans) to those seasons. In every year, there are thirteen of those moon cycles, each with twenty-eight days from one new moon to the next.

Many Native American people look at Turtle's back as a sort of calendar, with its pattern of thirteen large scales standing for the thirteen moons in each year. As Grandfather says to Sozap and as an Abenaki elder said to me long ago, it reminds us that all things are connected and we must try to live in balance.

Not all Native American people talk about twelve or thirteen moons. In some places, like the far north and the desert southwest, the seasons are divided, between winter and summer or between the dry time and the time of rains. Even when speaking of the moons, some Native American nations use several names for the same moon because so many things happen in the natural world at that time. Among the Potowatomi, for example, February is known not just as *Moon When Baby Bears Are Born*, but also *Moon of Snow*, and *Moon of the Wolves*. In this book, we have chosen just one moon story from each of thirteen Native American tribal nations in different regions of the continent to give a wider sense of the many things Native American people have been taught to notice in this beautiful world around us. It is a world which, as Sozap learned, must be listened to and respected.

J.B. and J.L.